A Note to Parents

Welcome to REAL KIDS READERS, a series of phonics-based books for children who are beginning to read. In the classroom, educators use phonics to teach children how to sound out unfamiliar words, providing a firm foundation for reading skills. At home, you can use REAL KIDS READERS to reinforce and build on that foundation, because the books follow the same basic phonic guidelines that children learn in school.

Of course the best way to help your child become a good reader is to make the experience fun—and REAL KIDS READERS do that, too. With their realistic story lines and lively characters, the books engage children's imaginations. With their clean design and sparkling photographs, they provide picture clues that help new readers decipher the text. The combination is sure to entertain young children and make them truly want to read.

REAL KIDS READERS have been developed at three distinct levels to make it easy for children to read at their own pace.

- LEVEL 1 is for children who are just beginning to read.
- LEVEL 2 is for children who can read with help.
- LEVEL 3 is for children who can read on their own.

A controlled vocabulary provides the framework at each level. Repetition, rhyme, and humor help increase word skills. Because children can understand the words and follow the stories, they quickly develop confidence. They go back to each book again and again, increasing their proficiency and sense of accomplishment, until they're ready to move on to the next level. The result is a rich and rewarding experience that will help them develop a lifelong love of reading.

For Anna Lewis,
who showed and taught me so much
—S. H.

Special thanks to Swatch for providing the watch and to
Morgenthal Frederics, New York City, for providing the eyeglasses.

Produced by DWAI / Seventeenth Street Productions, Inc.
Reading Specialist: Virginia Grant Clammer

Library of Congress Cataloging-in-Publication Data
Hood, Susan.
    Show and tell / Susan Hood ; photographs by Dorothy Handelman.
        p.   cm. — (Real kids readers. Level 2)
    Summary: A rhyming tale about a girl who forgets to bring something to school for
show-and-tell day.
    ISBN 0-7613-2056-3 (lib. bdg.). — ISBN 0-7613-2081-4 (pbk.)
    [1. Show-and-tell presentations—Fiction. 2. Schools—Fiction. 3. Stories in rhyme.]
I. Handelman, Dorothy, ill. II. Title. III. Series.
PZ8.3.H7577Sh   1999
[E]—dc21
                                                                98-34282
                                                                CIP
                                                                AC

pbk: 10 9 8 7 6 5 4 3 2 1
lib: 10 9 8 7 6 5 4 3 2 1

Show and Tell

By Susan Hood

Photographs by Dorothy Handelman

M
The Millbrook Press
Brookfield, Connecticut

My mom made me wear
these pants that I hate.
I missed the school bus,
so now I am late.

I bump Mrs. Wood.
Down goes her purse!
My day starts off badly,
and then it gets worse!

I groan when I hear
the other kids say,
"What did *you* bring in
for Show and Tell Day?"

Zack Burns has a bag,
and so does Sue Scott.
But I have no bag.
You see, I forgot.

I have nothing to show
and nothing to tell.
What will I do?
I do not feel well.

Sue has a seashell
she found by the shore.
If you hold it up close,
you can hear the sea roar.

I hear the sea roar
with the shell to my ear.
My tummy roars too.
Do the other kids hear?

Zack shows a bird's nest
he found in a tree.
The kids crowd around.
They all want to see.

Then it is Rick's turn.
He shows his loose tooth.
I smile when he says
his tooth has come "looth."

My turn will come soon.
Just two kids to go.
I have to get up
after Kate and Joe.

What can I show?
What can I tell?
When will this day end?
Did I hear the bell?

17

Kate shows a goose egg
she got on a farm.
I feel lots of goose bumps
pop up on my arm.

Joe shows his yo-yo,
but it will not work.
Now my turn is next.
I feel like a jerk.

The kids stare at me.
I sink in my chair.
I look in my desk—
no Show and Tell there.

I look in my pockets—
not one little thing.
The kids ask again,
"So what did you bring?"

23

My face feels red hot.
Then what do I see?
A mug and a spoon—
a SPOON will save me!

I ask Mrs. Wood,
"May I use your spoon?"
I tell her that I
will give it back soon.

I bet kids are thinking,
"That girl must be sick.
What good is a spoon?"
But I know a trick.

I place the spoon
on the end of my nose.
I stand very still
from my head to my toes.

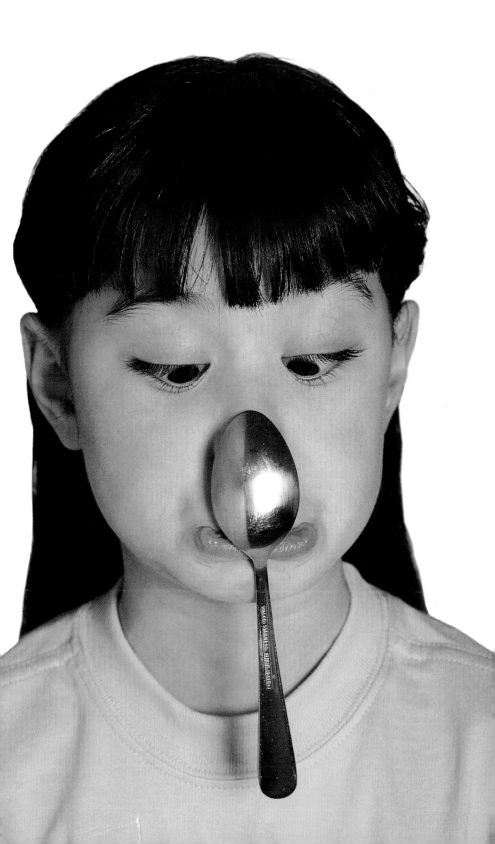

The kids clap and cheer.
They think I did well!
They say that my trick
was the best Show and Tell.

This day started badly.
It turned out okay.
Boy, am I glad
it was Show and Tell Day!

Phonic Guidelines

Use the following guidelines to help your child read the words in *Show and Tell*.

Short Vowels

When two consonants surround a vowel, the sound of the vowel is usually short. This means you pronounce *a* as in apple, *e* as in egg, *i* as in igloo, *o* as in octopus, and *u* as in umbrella. Short-vowel words in this story include: *bag, bet, bus, but, can, did, get, got, has, his, hot, kids, lots, mom, mug, not, pop, red, Tom's.*

Short-Vowel Words with Consonant Blends

When two or more different consonants are side by side, they usually blend to make a combined sound. In this story, short-vowel words with consonant blends include: *ask, best, bring, bump, clap, desk, end, glad, just, must, nest, next, pants, sink, stand, still.*

Double Consonants

When two identical consonants appear side by side, one of them is silent. In this story, double consonants appear in the short-vowel words *bell, egg, missed, Scott, shell, tell, well, will,* and in the *all*-family, the word *all.*

R-Controlled Vowels

When a vowel is followed by the letter *r,* its sound is changed by the *r.* In this story, words with *r*-controlled vowels include: *are, arm, bird's, Burns, farm, for, girl, her, jerk, purse, shore, starts, turn.*

Long Vowel and Silent E

If a word has a vowel and ends with an *e,* usually the vowel is long and the *e* is silent. Long vowels are pronounced the same way as their alphabet names. In this story, words with a long vowel and silent *e* include: *close, face, hate, late, like, made, nose, place, save, smile, use.*

Double Vowels

When two vowels are side by side, usually the first vowel is long and the second vowel is silent. Double-vowel words in this story include: *day, feel, groan, may, say, sea, see, toes, tree.*

Diphthongs

Sometimes when two vowels (or a vowel and a consonant) are side by side, they combine to make a diphthong—a sound that is different from long or short vowel sounds. Diphthongs are: *au/aw, ew, oi/oy, ou/ow.* In this story, words with diphthongs include: *around, boy, crowd, down, found, now.*

Consonant Digraphs

Sometimes when two different consonants are side by side, they make a digraph that represents a single new sound. Consonant digraphs are: *ch, sh, th, wh.* In this story, words with digraphs include: *that, then, there, these, they, thing, think, this, what, when, with.*

Silent Consonants

Sometimes when two different consonants appear side by side, one of them is silent. In this story, words with silent consonants include: *back, know, sick, trick, Zack.*

Sight Words

Sight words are those words that a reader must learn to recognize immediately—by sight—instead of by sounding them out. They occur with high frequency in easy texts. Sight words not included in the above categories are: *a, again, am, and, at, be, by, come, do, does, from, give, go, goes, good, have, he, hear, I, if, in, is, it, little, me, my, no, off, on, one, out, see, she, show, so, soon, the, to, too, two, up, very, want, was, you, your.*

This day started badly.
It turned out okay.
Boy, am I glad
it was Show and Tell Day!

Phonic Guidelines

Use the following guidelines to help your child read the words in *Show and Tell*.

Short Vowels

When two consonants surround a vowel, the sound of the vowel is usually short. This means you pronounce *a* as in apple, *e* as in egg, *i* as in igloo, *o* as in octopus, and *u* as in umbrella. Short-vowel words in this story include: *bag, bet, bus, but, can, did, get, got, has, his, hot, kids, lots, mom, mug, not, pop, red, Tom's.*

Short-Vowel Words with Consonant Blends

When two or more different consonants are side by side, they usually blend to make a combined sound. In this story, short-vowel words with consonant blends include: *ask, best, bring, bump, clap, desk, end, glad, just, must, nest, next, pants, sink, stand, still.*

Double Consonants

When two identical consonants appear side by side, one of them is silent. In this story, double consonants appear in the short-vowel words *bell, egg, missed, Scott, shell, tell, well, will,* and in the *all*-family, the word *all.*

R-Controlled Vowels

When a vowel is followed by the letter *r*, its sound is changed by the *r*. In this story, words with *r*-controlled vowels include: *are, arm, bird's, Burns, farm, for, girl, her, jerk, purse, shore, starts, turn.*

Long Vowel and Silent E

If a word has a vowel and ends with an *e*, usually the vowel is long and the *e* is silent. Long vowels are pronounced the same way as their alphabet names. In this story, words with a long vowel and silent *e* include: *close, face, hate, late, like, made, nose, place, save, smile, use.*

Double Vowels

When two vowels are side by side, usually the first vowel is long and the second vowel is silent. Double-vowel words in this story include: *day, feel, groan, may, say, sea, see, toes, tree.*

Diphthongs

Sometimes when two vowels (or a vowel and a consonant) are side by side, they combine to make a diphthong—a sound that is different from long or short vowel sounds. Diphthongs are: *au/aw, ew, oi/oy, ou/ow*. In this story, words with diphthongs include: *around, boy, crowd, down, found, now.*

Consonant Digraphs

Sometimes when two different consonants are side by side, they make a digraph that represents a single new sound. Consonant digraphs are: *ch, sh, th, wh*. In this story, words with digraphs include: *that, then, there, these, they, thing, think, this, what, when, with.*

Silent Consonants

Sometimes when two different consonants appear side by side, one of them is silent. In this story, words with silent consonants include: *back, know, sick, trick, Zack.*

Sight Words

Sight words are those words that a reader must learn to recognize immediately—by sight—instead of by sounding them out. They occur with high frequency in easy texts. Sight words not included in the above categories are: *a, again, am, and, at, be, by, come, do, does, from, give, go, goes, good, have, he, hear, I, if, in, is, it, little, me, my, no, off, on, one, out, see, she, show, so, soon, the, to, too, two, up, very, want, was, you, your.*